Meet the staff of

THE TREEHOUSE TIMES

AMY—The neighborhood newspaper is Amy's most brilliant idea ever—a perfect project for her and her friends, with a perfect office location—the treehouse in Amy's backyard!

ERIN—A great athlete despite her tiny size, Erin will be a natural when it comes to covering any sports-related story in the town of Kirkridge.

LEAH—Tall and thin with long, dark hair and blue eyes, Leah is the artistic-type. She hates drawing attention to herself, but with her fashion-model looks, it's impossible not to.

ROBIN—With her bright red hair, freckles and green eyes, and a loud chirpy voice, nobody can miss Robin—and Robin misses nothing when it comes to getting a good story.

Keep Your Nose in the News with
THE TREEHOUSE TIMES Series
by Page McBrier

PAGE McBRIER grew up in Indianapolis, Indiana, and St. Louis, Missouri, in a large family with lots of pets. In college she studied children's theater and later taught drama in California and New York. She currently lives in Rowayton, Connecticut, with her husband, Peter Morrison, a film producer, and their two small sons.

THE TREEHOUSE TIMES

#9

Stinky Business

Page McBrier

THE TREEHOUSE TIMES #9: STINKY BUSINESS is an original publication of Avon Books. This work has never before appeared in book form.

AVON BOOKS
A division of
The Hearst Corporation
105 Madison Avenue
New York, New York 10016

Published by arrangement with the author
Library of Congress Catalog Card Number: 90-93389
ISBN: 0-380-76269-2
RL: 4.8

First Avon Camelot Printing: January 1991

Printed in the U.S.A.

OPM 10 9 8 7 6 5 4 3 2 1

For Mom and Dad

THE TREEHOUSE TIMES

#9

Stinky Business

Chapter One

"Yuck. What do you think it is?" Twelve-year-old Amy Evans stood on the sandy riverbank, straining her eyes at the soggy, furry lump she could see wedged between a rock and a fallen tree branch further downstream.

Beside her, Amy's best friend Erin Valdez wrinkled her dark eyebrows and tried to peer past the rocks and around the next bend. "I'm not sure from here. A muskrat, maybe?"

Amy stooped down to pick up another beer can, tossing it into her nearly full garbage bag. "A muskrat? In Kirkridge?" Kirkridge, the town in which they lived, was actually a suburb of St. Louis.

"Or it could be a raccoon," said Erin. "This part of the Meramec River has both." As she leaned all ninety pounds of herself dangerously out over the stream for a better view, another group of kids, all wearing OPERATION CLEAN STREAM T-shirts, began noisily rolling a large, mossy tire out of the water and up the slope.

"Maybe we should just leave the poor thing alone to rot in peace," Amy heard herself saying aloud. "It can't be polluting the river any more than the rest of this junk."

Beside them their friend, Robin Ryan, looked relieved. "I wouldn't touch a dead animal if I were you. It could have rabies or something."

Erin grinned and handed Amy the large plastic bag she'd been using to collect trash. "Nothing dead has rabies, Robin," she said, stepping onto a large, wobbly rock.

Robin got a worried expression on her face. "Wait. Where are you going?"

"To get a closer look," said Erin, leaping like a mountain goat along the shoreline. "Dad might be able to use it in his classroom . . . whatever it is." Dead animals had never bothered Erin. She came from the kind of family that took no-frills camping trips for vacations.

"What if you slip and fall in?"

"It's not that deep," said Erin, grabbing a tree branch like Tarzan and swinging herself out onto a gravel sandbar.

Today was Emerson Park's official spring clean-up day, and Amy and her friends Erin, Robin, and Leah Fox were here to cover the action for their neighborhood newspaper, the *Treehouse Times*.

Amy's eyes swept along the stretch of the shoreline they'd been assigned to cover. From where she was standing at the moment, the river actually looked more like a wide stream, about half the length of a football field, with banks sloping to a sandy gravel bar.

They watched Erin pick her way over to where the dead animal was stuck. "It's a muskrat," she shouted.

"Are you sure it's dead?" Amy yelled back.

"Positive," she said. "I'm taking it to Dad."

"Forget it," said Robin. "I'm not carrying

that thing anywhere. I thought we were down here to do a story."

Erin shouted, "Does anyone see something we can carry it on?"

"It's too waterlogged to dissect," said Robin. "Isn't it?"

Amy's eyes skimmed across the littered sandbar on which they were standing and landed on a large piece of dirty cardboard. "What about this?" she said, holding it up and waving it.

Just then Leah, the newspaper's photographer, appeared. "You wouldn't believe what someone just found farther down," she said. "A whole refrigerator! It still had food inside it. I got a great picture of a jar of pickles in the inside door." She noticed the rest of them watching Erin. "What's she doing down there?"

"Rescuing a dead muskrat," said Robin.

"Gross."

Downstream, Erin began waving her arms excitedly. "You guys! You guys!"

"What is it?" called Amy.

"I found something else." She pried the muskrat loose and dangled it in the air.

"I hope she remembers to wash her hands," said Leah.

"Look!" said Erin, shaking the animal back and forth. "It's wearing a collar."

Robin sniffed. "Who'd want a muskrat for a pet?"

Erin hopped with the muskrat back to where they were standing and dropped it with a wet plop onto the bank. "For your information, this is no pet. See this ID tag? That means it's being studied."

"By whom?" said Amy.

"A biologist," said Erin. She knelt down and twisted the small silver collar tag until it caught the light. "Number 1140753."

"That's helpful," said Leah.

"Maybe your dad would know who's studying muskrats around here," said Amy to Erin. Erin's father was the biology teacher at Kirkridge High.

"He might," said Erin, surveying the shore. She poked at the muskrat with a stick. "Poor little guy." She rolled him onto the sheet of cardboard and gingerly lifted it.

"Where are you going?" said Leah.

"Home," said Erin. "We've filled all our trash bags, haven't we?"

"But I wanted to do some more interviews," said Amy. The newspaper came out once a month, and this month, in honor of

Earth Day, they'd decided to focus on the environment, tying it in with today's park and river clean-up.

The muskrat wobbled like a Jell-O mold on top of the cardboard. "If I hang around too long, this thing's going to stink," warned Erin.

"Okay, okay," said Amy, stepping out of Erin's way. "Call me later." She turned back to Leah, who was taking a picture of Robin standing beside their four giant trash bags. "Show me where you found that refrigerator," she said. "Maybe there's a ranger or someone who wants to talk about it."

Amy had nearly forgotten the muskrat when Erin phoned her at home that night. "I found out who Chester belongs to," she said to Amy.

"Who's Chester?"

"The muskrat," said Erin. "Dad traced the tag to the Parks Department. They're doing a survey on aquatic animals."

"Oh," said Amy politely.

"Want to go with me when I return him? I can't go tomorrow because of soccer practice, but maybe the next day."

Amy hesitated. "Has he started to stink?"

"Not yet. I put him in a paper bag in the freezer. Anyway, the lab should be interesting. Maybe we can get more stuff for our Earth Day issue."

"Like what?"

"I don't know. They do all sorts of interesting things at the Parks Department. Their lab is right there in Emerson Park."

Amy smiled. Leave it to Erin to get excited about the Parks Department. "Okay. But don't let Chester thaw out until we're ready to leave."

Erin laughed. "Don't worry. I won't."

The next day in study hall, Amy was working on an essay for English class, "The Bare Bones of the Earth," when she felt a tap on her shoulder and heard a deep voice behind her say, "Amy Evans. I have a proposal for you."

She looked up to see Grant Taylor—neighbor, friend, and science genius, not necessarily in that order—leaning over her with a smile as wide as the Mississippi. "Remember that science contest I won last fall?"

Amy grinned back. "You mean the two hundred dollars you got, thanks to me?" If Amy hadn't secretly entered Grant's mousetrap contraption into the contest, he'd never have won first prize.

"Shh," said the girl sitting next to Amy. "This is supposed to be study hall."

Grant grabbed a chair and pulled it up beside Amy's. "You see," he said, sitting so close that their knees touched, "I planned to use the money to build a weather station on my parents' roof but now they said it's too dangerous. I need to find another location." He started up with the smile again.

"Wait a second," said Amy. "You're not thinking of . . ."

"The treehouse!" said Grant. "My instruments would be protected and I'd be off the ground."

"But that's our office!" The treehouse had originally been built by Amy's father and her brother, Patrick, as a place for Patrick to stay out of trouble. Once Patrick grew *out* of trees and *into* girls and motorcycles, though, he passed it along to Amy, who transformed it into a newspaper office.

"There's still plenty of room," said Grant, his logic cranking forward like a bulldozer. "I promise I'll stay out of the way."

Amy couldn't imagine Grant staying out of anything's way, even if he wanted to, but she didn't want to hurt his feelings, so instead she said, "I have to talk to the others first."

"Wait," said Grant. "There's more. I don't just want to *use* your treehouse. I plan to give you something in return." Grant had the strangest way of working one idea into another. "What if I did a weather forecast for each issue? We could call it 'Grant's Almanac'!"

Amy lifted her eyebrows. "The paper only comes out once a month, Grant. A month is a long time to wait for a weather report."

"I can still make predictions and forecasts," he said. "C'mon! The paper needs some new blood. It's always the same people, writing the same way."

Amy stopped. "You think?"

"When's the last time you assigned an outsider to do a different kind of feature?"

"Well," said Amy slowly. "There was Daphne and her advice column. . . ."

"That was last summer."

"True." The final bell rang. "We don't ever write the same kind of stuff, though. Our next issue is going to be really interesting. It's on the environment."

Before Amy had a chance to grab her

books, Grant picked them up and loaded them on top of his own. "All the more reason," he said, walking into the hall, "to include a weather forecast."

It happened that the regular weekly meeting of the *Treehouse Times* was scheduled later that same afternoon, after Erin's soccer practice. As soon as Amy got home, she tried to figure out how to fit Grant's weather station into the treehouse, since it was all Grant talked about on the bus ride home. One of his charms was a one-track mind.

She stood at the kitchen door, squinting up at the treehouse. If it weren't in a tree, it would probably be called a playhouse, since it had walls, a roof, windows, and even curtains, sewn by Robin's mother a year ago.

"What are you staring at?" asked Patrick, sneaking up from behind.

"Grant wants to put a weather station in the treehouse," she said.

"That's cool," said Patrick. Lately, everything was cool to Patrick.

"I don't know," said Amy. "Have you ever seen the way he keeps his room? It's really messy. What if he gets into our things, or what if he lets Roddy come visit him?"

Roddy was Roddy Casper, Amy's wormy neighbor and Grant's best friend.

Patrick's head bobbed up and down as if he were keeping time with a drum. "Yeah."

Amy looked out at the tree again. "I mean, I like Grant and all that, don't misunderstand me. He's a genius when it comes to inventions. Someday he'll probably invent something that makes him a millionaire, and I bet he won't change his lifestyle one bit. He'll still sleep on an old mattress under his desk and live on Big Macs."

"Yeah," said Patrick, staring into space.

Amy made a face. "Patrick! What is *with* you?"

"Heather Hartford," he said, nodding nonstop. "Second period English."

"Is she the one with the skinny legs?"

"That's Leslie," said Patrick. "Heather has long, red hair."

"Oh, that one," said Amy. "The one you were talking to in front of the house yesterday."

"She was on her way to her piano lesson. Do you believe it? A babe like her taking piano lessons!"

Amy shook her head. "She probably missed it, you talked so long. So do you think we should let Grant share the tree-house?''

Patrick gave her a blank look. ''Why would you want to do that?''

''Never mind,'' said Amy. ''Never mind.''

Amy brought up Grant's idea first thing when their meeting started later. ''I didn't say yes; I said we'd vote on it.''

''I like the idea of a weather almanac,'' said Erin.

''Me, too,'' said Leah, who liked anything out of the ordinary. ''We won't know if the idea works until we try it.''

''True,'' said Amy.

Robin, who had been concentrating on the Oreos until now, suddenly said, ''Grant's right about never having anyone else write for the paper, you know. Ever since Daphne, we've done all the work ourselves.''

Amy's eyes narrowed. ''I didn't think that was a problem, Robin. It's our paper. We each have our assignments.''

Robin groped inside the Oreo bag for the last cookie. ''I know. But why couldn't we turn one of our regular columns into a guest column, for variety. Each month we could ask a different person . . .''

"The movie column!" interrupted Erin. "We could feature a different reviewer each month!"

"Yeah!" said Robin, forgetting the cookies. "We could ask neighbors, teachers . . . just about anyone."

"Okay," said Amy, warming up to the idea. "Who should we ask first? It has to be someone willing to write."

"I have this friend from Sunday School named Kelly Livingston," said Robin. "She goes to Westlake, and she's on the school paper. Her dad's our minister."

"Great!" said Amy. "Ask her if she'd like to start our guest movie reviews."

"Okay," said Robin.

"What about Grant?" said Erin. "Have we decided to let him set up his weather station?"

Amy looked around at her friends. "What do you think?"

"He *can* be a pig," said Robin.

Leah began braiding a strand of her long, dark hair. "Maybe we can offer him a thirty-day trial, like they do with hair gels. If we're not satisfied, we can return him."

"Yeah!" said Robin, Queen of the Slobs. "We find one potato chip on the floor and he's out!" She looked at the others and swallowed. "Just kidding."

Amy smiled, secretly pleased Grant was being given a chance. "I'll tell him he's got thirty days to prove himself."

"Thirty days," said Erin. "I sure hope he can do it."

Chapter Two

That night Amy was in bed, having a great dream about a school field trip to Disney World, when she was jarred out of her sleep by a loud pounding. As she lay there, trying to forget the noise so she could get back to her dream, Patrick burst into her room.

"Next time knock, please," she said. Disney World faded away.

Patrick gave her a sarcastic look. "Why? No one important is in here. Did you hear your boyfriend hammering outside?"

"What boyfriend? I don't have a boyfriend."

Patrick gave an obnoxious smile. "Grant.

Sounds like he'd doing some remodeling in the treehouse."

Amy jerked up her head. "What!" she screeched. She groped for her glasses, looked at her clock, then jumped out of bed and grabbed her jeans from the back of her desk chair. "Why isn't he asleep like normal people?" She stared at Patrick, who obviously thought the whole thing was hilarious. "Do you mind? I have to get dressed."

As Patrick slid out of the room he said, "Take your time. Dad already went out there."

Amy gulped. "He did?" She thought about running to the window to watch until she remembered she was in her pajamas. "Is he mad?"

"Do I look like a mind reader?"

"Never mind," said Amy, shoving him on his way.

All seemed quiet in treehouse-land when Amy hurried outside a few minutes later. She saw her father standing on the ground and waving his flashlight at Grant, who was in the Crow's Nest above the main part of the treehouse. "What's going on?" she asked in as casual a voice as she could manage.

"I'm installing my hygrometer," said Grant, like it made perfect sense to be working up there at eleven o'clock at night. He bent back over his whatever-it-was and did a few more adjustments. "Almost finished."

Amy's father swung the beam of the flashlight back onto the lawn. "Amy," he whispered, "is this something that could have waited?"

"I'm not sure," she said truthfully. "I told him he could put his weather station up there."

"Done!" called Grant. He squeezed through the ceiling hatch, tossing his tools with a loud clunk onto the treehouse floor. "Is there any way these hatches can be widened?" he asked, shoving himself through the bottom one, then leaping like a big gorilla onto the ground.

"No," said Amy.

It felt weird to be standing in the backyard in the middle of the night with Grant and her father. She wasn't sure what to say, so she was glad when her father spoke up. "So," he said, turning to Grant, "did you finish your work, son?" Son of Frankenstein is more like it, thought Amy, glaring up at Grant's moon-sized head.

"Yes, sir," Grant said, focusing on a clump of grass at his feet.

"What exactly is a hygrometer?"

"It measures moisture."

Mr. Evans nodded, then said, "Ah, tell me something. Is it necessary to do this type of installation at night?"

"Nope." Grant shifted his eyes from the ground to the treehouse. "I just like working at night. So did Thomas Edison."

"I see," said her father. He paused. "Do you foresee any more projects that require pounding?"

"A couple."

"Maybe you could do them in the afternoon," interrupted Amy, "*so you don't wake anyone up.*"

Thomas Edison's light bulb must have finally gone off in Grant's head. "Oh! Sorry. Were you sleeping, Mr. Evans?"

"No," he said. "But your hammering was disturbing the neighborhood."

"Oh," said Grant a second time. Without even a good-bye, he started off toward his house, then stopped suddenly, as if he'd just remembered something. "I was thinking of enlarging the observation platform some."

"You were?" said Amy.

"See what the others think," he quickly added.

"Okay," said Amy, who was already wondering if she'd made a bad mistake, giving Grant permission. "We'll talk about it tomorrow afternoon."

The next morning at the bus stop Erin said to Amy, "Want to return Chester today?"

"You still have that thing?" Robin butted in. "Why didn't your dad chop it up?"

Erin gave her a dirty look. "He doesn't dissect everything, Robin. Besides, Chester has to go back to the Parks Department."

"Want to come with us?" asked Amy. "I bet we get some great stuff for our environment issue."

Amy looked at Robin, then Erin. If it weren't for the paper, the two of them would never have been friends. Robin was messy and undependable, but the world's greatest snoop. She could worm things out of people like no one else. Erin, on the other hand, was a model of neatness and dependability. Amy counted on her, which was important if you were running a newspaper.

"I guess I could," said Robin. "Where is it?"

"Emerson Park," said Amy. "We'll have to ride our bikes." The park, which covered about forty acres, was located on the edge of Kirkridge and bordered the Meramec River. Amy had never spent much time there, except for an occasional family picnic, before they decided to do this environment issue. Now she turned to Erin and said, "Is there someone special we're supposed to see?"

Erin started laughing. "A guy named Lief Hopper."

"Very funny," said Robin.

"I'm not joking," said Erin, totally cracking up. "He's a biologist for the Parks Department."

"Are you sure?" said Amy, immediately feeling sorry for him. "That's his real name? Leaf hopper?"

"Swear on a stack of Bibles," said Erin.

"Oh boy," said Robin. "Now I *really* can't wait to go. Where do you want to meet?"

"How about my house?" said Erin. "Four o'clock." She looked directly at Robin. "And don't be late."

Erin poked at the brown paper bag lying between her and Amy on the lawn. "He's thawing," she said. "I can feel him through the bag."

"Oh, ick," said Amy.

"Why did you have to invite Robin anyway?" said Erin. "She's always late."

"Not always," said Amy. "Besides, she's a good reporter." She rolled up her pants legs to take advantage of the warm sun. "I'm sure she has a good excuse."

Erin glanced at her new sports watch. "I say we give her ten more minutes, then leave. Chester's not happy about waiting."

At that moment, Amy saw Robin hurrying up the block toward them. Even from far away, she could tell Robin had been crying. Her face, normally freckled and rosy, was covered with giant red blotches. "Sorry I'm late," she mumbled. "Elvis escaped." Elvis was the Ryans' spoiled-rotten parakeet. Since it was the only pet their dad allowed them to have, they let it fly all over the house and eat food off people's plates and poop wherever it wanted. Amy thought it was totally disgusting, but she knew Robin really loved Elvis, so she tried hard to be sympathetic.

"How did he get out?" said Amy.

Robin burst into tears. "It's all my fault. I left the door to his cage open so he could get some exercise and Hilary didn't know he was out and opened the window. I've been calling for him in the backyard this whole time, but I don't think he heard me." She started up with the tears again. "What's he going to eat? How's he going to stay warm at night?"

"Don't worry," said Erin. "I bet when he gets hungry he'll come back. Leave a little cup of birdseed for him on the window."

Robin sniffed. "Elvis doesn't eat birdseed. He likes croissants with peanut butter, and Pop Tarts."

Erin rolled her eyes. "Do you want us to help you look for him?"

"Would you?" said Robin. She must have really been concerned since she jammed about six caramel chewies into her mouth at once.

"Wait a second," said Amy. "What about

Lief Hopper?" She glanced down at the paper bag. "And Chester?"

"How long can it take?" said Erin. She stood up and brushed the dirt off the back of her jeans. Although she'd never admit it, she always put animals and pets (and soccer practice) before people. It was part of her outdoorsy personality. "Maybe a few Pop Tarts would help," she said to Robin. "Come on. Let's try."

They sat in Robin's yard for almost an hour, as Chester got softer and softer. Erin tried every trick she could think of to coax Elvis back, but he stayed out of sight. It was getting late, and Amy was glad when Erin finally said, "Maybe if we leave for a while and then come back, he'll have found his own way home."

"Think so?" said Robin.

"I do," said Amy. "Once it gets dark and he realizes he can't find peanut butter in trees, he'll show up."

Robin wiped a tear from her cheek. "Okay. I hope you're right."

The Parks Department stood near the river in a building that looked like a giant corrugated toolshed. Out front, a couple of beatup pickup trucks were parked beside an old gasoline pump. On the front door was a SAVE OUR EARTH bumper sticker.

"Should we knock?" said Amy, trying to see inside. "It's pretty late. Maybe they've all gone home."

"It looks to me like the kind of door you just open," said Robin, who had lightened up a little after they stopped for ice-cream bars.

Amy turned the handle and let them all in. Toward the back of the room she noticed some lab counters with equipment on them. To the right was an old wooden desk piled high with papers. A couple of wire traps, the kind that didn't kill animals, were stacked on the floor to the left. "Hello, anybody here?" called Amy.

No answer.

Robin giggled. "Oh, leaf hopper," she sang. "Come out, come out, wherever you are!"

"Shhh!" said Erin. "What if he hears you?"

"May I help you?" said a man's voice behind them.

"Eeek!" screamed Robin.

A tall man with a red beard and crinkly eyes smiled. "Were you looking for me?" he said to Robin.

Her face turned redder than his beard.

He stuck out his hand. "Lief Hopper."

"Nice to meet you," mumbled Robin, giving him a limp shake. She introduced the others.

"What can I do for you girls?" He was dressed in a plaid shirt and blue jeans like Paul Bunyan's.

"We found this muskrat in the river during the park clean-up," said Erin, unwrapping Chester, who was completely thawed now. "He has your tag on him."

Mr. Hopper took the muskrat in his hands and turned him over slowly. "Hmm. Thanks. He's part of my aquatic-animal study." They followed him over to a large freezer, where he put Chester to rest with an assortment of other creatures—birds, fish, and larger animals.

When Robin saw the little frozen birds she made a choking noise, probably because they reminded her of Elvis.

"What's going to happen to him?" said Erin, as if Chester had become part of her family.

"I'll run some tests on him," said Mr. Hopper. He gave Erin a curious look. "How'd you know he was ours?"

"My dad teaches biology at Kirkridge High."

"Uh, Mr. Hopper," interrupted Amy.

He leaned down. "Who?"

"Mr. Hopper?"

He winked. "Call me Lief. Mr. Hopper is my father."

"Okay," said Amy. She blushed. "We have a neighborhood newspaper called the *Treehouse Times* and it comes out once a month. This month we want to feature Earth Day and do an environmental issue." She took a deep breath.

"Great idea," said Lief.

"We already helped with the river cleanup last weekend . . ." said Amy.

"And we were wondering what you do down here," said Erin, finishing the sentence.

From her jeans pocket, Amy pulled out her reporter's notebook.

Lief thought for a minute. "Well, I'm what they call an urban biologist. I study ecological issues that affect city environments."

Robin squinched up her eyes. "Like what?"

"Like the river out there. I focus on how it's affected by pollution and other things in the atmosphere."

"Is it very polluted?" asked Erin.

"Yes and no," said Lief. "Take the fish, for example. The bottom fish—catfish and carp—suffer from chlordane contamination. Chlordane is what people use to treat termites in their homes. What happens is that the chlordane seeps into the soil and then makes its way down to the river, where it's absorbed by the plants and debris that the bottom fish feed on. The other fish—bass, bluegill—aren't affected since they don't feed on bottom matter."

"Wait a second," said Amy. "I remember seeing some signs down there about not eating the catfish because of the contamination."

"That's right," he said. "If enough of it gets into a person, it can start affecting the nervous system, among other things."

"But doesn't the chlorine taste bad?" asked Robin.

"Chlordane," said Lief. "You can't taste it."

"Then how do you know it's there?" said Amy.

"We run periodic tests on the fish," said Lief.

"Cool!" said Erin. "Could we watch sometime?"

Lief nodded and stroked his beard. "I don't see why not. If you'd like, you can come out in the field with me this Saturday to collect sample specimens."

"Wow. That would make a great story," said Amy. "Is it all right if our photographer comes with us?"

He nodded. "Sure. All I ask is that you respect the river and give a hand when I need it."

"That sounds easy," said Erin, ready to go. "What time should we meet you?"

Lief rubbed his hands together. "I like to get an early start . . . say seven o'clock."

Robin groaned. "Seven o'clock!"

"We'll be here," said Amy firmly. "See you then."

By the time they were back in their neighborhood, it was nearly dark. "I'd better get home," said Amy. "My parents are probably wondering where I am."

"Mine, too," said Erin.

Robin stopped her bike. "Wait! Aren't you going to help me look for Elvis?"

"He's probably home by now," said Erin.

Robin looked traumatized. "Please? You promised."

Erin hesitated.

"Please?" said Robin.

Erin turned her wheels. "Okay. I guess I can call Mom to let her know where I am."

"Me, too," said Amy, not wanting to desert Erin. "Anyway, I bet Elvis has already found his way back to your windowsill."

When they'd left Robin's house earlier, the girls had put the bird's cage with the door propped open on the windowsill. Now they walked into Robin's kitchen and the first person they met was Robin's mother, Queen of the Worrywarts.

"What happened to Elvis?" she said. "How did he get out?"

"Isn't he back yet?" said Robin.

"I warned you this could happen if you weren't careful," said Robin's mother.

"Mom! I didn't do it on purpose! It was an accident!"

Mrs. Ryan pursed her lips. "What's going

to become of him? He can't survive out there!"

While Mrs. Ryan was making Robin feel guilty, Erin picked up a soggy Pop Tart and went to stand outside the window, where she began calling softly, "Here birdie, birdie," making little kissing sounds. "Come on home, Elvis."

From one of the trees, there was a sudden flapping noise as Elvis swooped past Erin and back up into the tree. "He's here!" she screamed. "I saw him."

Robin and her mother ran to the window. "Where?" asked Robin.

"He just dive-bombed me," said Erin.She waved the Pop Tart in the air. "Let me try again. Here, Elvis. Here, boy."

This time, Elvis came in for a landing . . . on top of Erin's head. "Whoa," said Erin, trying to remain calm.

"Elvis! Thank God you're back," said Mrs. Ryan. "Erin, let him nibble on the Pop Tart and turn around so he sees his cage."

Erin rotated slowly.

"Look!" said Amy. "He's got something shiny in his beak."

"What is it?" said Erin, turning her eyes upward.

"I'm not sure," said Amy. Elvis hopped off Erin's head and into the cage.

"Gotcha!" said Robin, slamming the door. She peered inside. "It's an earring," she reported, re-opening the door and fishing it out. She held up a round, silver dangle, set with three purple stones. "Isn't it pretty?" She started to try it on.

"Robin! What are you doing?" said her mother. "That earring has been in the bird's mouth!"

Robin stuck the earring in place, saying, "It's okay, Mom. Elvis is healthy."

"But you don't know where it's been before that, or who it belonged to," said her mother.

Amy stared at the earring. "Wait a second," she interrupted. "I've seen that earring somewhere."

"You have?" said Erin. "Where?"

Amy tried as hard as she could to remember. "I'm not sure. It was recently, though."

"Hmm," said Erin. "Maybe we can run an ad for it in the paper."

"Maybe," said Amy. Where *had* she seen that earring? Surely, by the time the paper was published, she would remember.

Chapter Three

It was so late by the time Amy got home that she'd missed supper—not that supper around her house was any big deal. Her mother often worked late at the realty agency where she was office manager, so the rest of them had learned to fend for themselves. Amy didn't really mind—her mother's cooking wasn't going to win any Betty Crocker awards anyway. She poured herself a bowl of cereal and sprinkled some raisins on top.

Her father wandered in wearing his old blue sweats, the ones he wore when he was doing repairs around the house. "Hi Dad," she said. "Where is everyone?"

"Your mother had a realty board meeting and Patrick is out."

"Out?"

He sighed. "That's all he would tell me and I didn't want to seem like a meddling father, especially since he'd finished his homework for once. All I know is he took his second shower for the day and changed clothes."

"Heather Hartford," said Amy.

"Who?"

"Some girl he likes."

Her father tilted his head. "Don't *you* ever turn funny on me, okay?"

"Patrick isn't funny, Dad."

Her father gave her a sad smile. "We used to *do* things together. . . ."

"Don't worry, Dad. It's only puberty."

Mr. Evans started to laugh. "Great," he said. "You mean there's more coming?"

Amy felt herself blushing. "I guess there is. I hadn't thought of it that way."

The next afternoon Amy decided to do her homework up in the treehouse since it was such a pretty day. She tossed her books and a can of soda into her backpack and took off, but even before she got halfway, she could see she wasn't going to be alone.

"Hi Grant," she called, trying not to look too disappointed at having company.

"Come on up," he said. His T-shirt was soaked with sweat.

"Uh, okay," said Amy. "But I can only stay a minute."

She poked her head through the hatch. On top of her desk sat a large glass cylinder with a funnel on top. The floor was littered with rubber tubing, glass test tubes, and duct tape. Grant was busy nailing a long thermometer to the wall.

Amy surveyed the mess cautiously. "Gosh. What is all this stuff?"

He pointed to Amy's desk. "Hygrometer." Then the floor. "Cape Cod barometer." Then the wall. "Thermometer." He leaned over to read it. "Sixty-two degrees."

"Doesn't feel that warm," she said, feeling a little overwhelmed by all of Grant's weather equipment.

Grant grunted. "If you want to know the wind direction or velocity, the weather vane and wind-speed meter are up in the Crow's Nest." He wiped a big glob of sweat off his neck, causing Amy to notice the muscle in his right arm. "I had the hygrometer up there, too, but I decided to move it down here where it'll stay dry." He leaned out the window and stared up at the sky. "Rain's coming tonight. It's going to rain the rest of the week."

"Wow," she said. "Did you predict that on your instruments?"

Grant grinned. "No. I heard it on the radio."

"Grant!" She laughed and then looked nervously around the room. "Are you planning to . . . you know . . . add any more stuff?"

"Just my recording charts," said Grant. "I thought I'd use that wall over there." He waved his arm, the one holding the hammer, and Amy ducked, just to be safe.

"Sounds good," she said, straightening back up. She paused. "You're going to uh, clean all this up when you're finished, right?"

"Sure." He began his hammering again. "Come back later if you don't believe me."

"That's okay," said Amy, getting drowned out by the hammering. "I believe you. I think."

Grant was right about the rain. For the rest of the week it poured, causing her to wonder whether they'd be able to go out on the river with Lief on Saturday. But Friday evening, things suddenly cleared up and the trip to the river began to look more promising.

Amy's alarm went off at six A.M. the next morning. After she shut it off, she groped around for her glasses, then sat up to listen to the birds chirping. Clear, pale sunlight poured through the window. A perfect day.

Erin was waiting for Amy in front of her house when Amy rode up not long afterward. They'd arranged to meet Leah and Robin at the lab. "Come on!" said Amy, who was so excited she didn't even want to slow down her pedaling.

Erin took a flying jump and landed on her bike. "We're out of here!" she shouted, loud enough to wake the neighborhood.

As they pedaled up to the lab, they could see Robin and Leah waiting for them on the front steps. "How did you get here so soon?" asked Amy.

Robin looked embarrassed. "Mom brought us. She didn't want me riding my bike through the park this early."

Amy looked around. "Is Lief here?"

"He's getting his gear ready," said Robin.

"Morning," said Lief, coming around from

the side of the building. He was carrying a large fishing net and a bucket and had on tall rubber boots that stretched past his knees.

"God," whispered Leah. "All he needs is a bowl of granola."

Lief got right to the point. "It shouldn't take us long to collect our samples. After we're finished, we'll come back and run these suckers through their paces." He squinted up at the sun. "Well, let's get going."

He led them along a back path, through a forest of tall trees and down to the river's edge. "This feels like a Girl Scout hike," said Robin, picking her way through the mud.

"Watch out for the wildflowers over there," said Lief. He pointed to a quiet pool of water. "I usually have good luck right here." Steadying himself with a tree branch, he eased his boots into the water. "Someone hand me my net." The water came just below his boots.

As Amy passed it over, she said to Leah, "Are you getting pictures of this?" Sometimes Leah got so absorbed in watching something that she forgot why she was there.

"Oh, yeah," she said, pulling the lens cap off her camera.

Lief dipped the net into the water and waited.

"How did you learn to do this?" asked Erin.

"Indians," he said, grinning. He suddenly became very still. Swoosh! With a quick motion, he jerked the net into the air. "Got one!"

"Wow," said Erin. "Even the Indians weren't that fast!"

Inside the net, a big, slimy catfish slithered and squirmed. "Someone fill that bucket with water," instructed Lief. As soon as it was full, he plopped the catfish inside.

"Eeeeuuu," said Robin, bending over to watch. The catfish's tail slapped rhythmically against the sides of the pail and then it rolled onto its back and opened its wide mouth. "What's going to happen to him?" Robin asked, wrinkling her nose.

Lief sloshed the fish around in the pail. "He gets sacrificed in the name of scientific research."

"I was afraid you were going to say that."

Lief looked out at the river. "In my opinion, it's a shame we have to monitor the river at all."

"Is this part of the river getting cleaner or dirtier?" asked Amy.

Lief thought for a minute. "Overall, I'd say cleaner, thanks to all the programs we have to educate people today. But it's always an uphill battle." He turned back to his fishing. "Excuse me, will you?"

It didn't take long to get the rest of the samples—another catfish and a couple of carp. When the bucket was full, Lief waded over to have a look. "Hmm," he said.

"What is it?" asked Amy.

Lief poked at one of the carp with his finger. "They seem a little sluggish, that's all." He waded out of the water. "Ready to go back to the lab?"

"What happens next?" asked Amy.

"Test time," said Lief, grabbing the bucket and striding off. They had to run to catch up.

"What made you become a biologist?" asked Amy, as they headed for the lab.

"I don't know," said Lief. "I always liked being outdoors, studying the environment." He turned his head. "What made you become a journalist?"

"She's nosy," said Robin, leaping a huge puddle.

"Look who's talking," said Amy with a laugh.

When they reached the lab, Lief took them in the back way. A woman wearing a white lab coat was bent over a microscope. "Hi, Susan," Lief said.

She looked over at him. "Girl Scouts?"

"Nope. Reporters." He led them over to a large metal instrument. "This," he said, "is a mass spectrometer." He spelled it out so they'd have it right. "We use it to screen for inorganic substances . . . the bad guys." He picked up a large hammer. "Now turn your backs, please." They obediently faced the other way. Amy heard a loud thunk. "Okay, you can turn around again," he said, placing a very dead catfish onto the lab table.

"Ick," said Robin.

"It goes downhill from here," said Lief. "If you want to leave, you can." No one did, though.

Using a pair of pliers, Lief quickly skinned the catfish, then filleted it, just like they would do at a fish store. Then he took a piece of the fish and placed it in a small glass bowl. "I'm going to add a clear solution to break down the cell walls,'' he told them, pouring it in. ''Now we mash until it becomes liquid.''

Leah and Robin, the two with weak stomachs, started looking a little pale.

''I'm almost done, but you can step outside if you need air.'' He did a few more mashes then said, ''Now we inject some of this into our spectrometer and ask the equipment to check for chlordane.'' He spun some dials and made some adjustments. ''There you are,'' he said. From the desk drawer he took out a chart. ''This is where I record the levels.''

''Has it gotten higher?'' asked Amy.

''About the same.''

''If you were going to test for something else, would you do it the same way?'' asked Erin.

''Sure,'' said Lief. ''I'd just have to tell the mass spectrometer what we were looking for.'' He took some more of their sample. ''I'll show you. Let's pretend we're looking for methyl mercury, which is a highly toxic form of mercury found in fish and plants.''

''What's toxic mean?'' asked Robin.

''Poisonous.''

She gasped. "These fish have poison in them?"

"They shouldn't," he said. "We test for mercury yearly on this part of the river." He injected the solution and made the adjustments. The test went through its paces. "Hmm," he said, staring at the screen.

"What is it?" said Amy.

Lief took another sample and ran it through.

"Did you see something?" asked Erin.

He lifted his head. His lips were set in a straight line. "Susan, can you come here a minute? I want you to look at this reading."

When Susan looked at the screen her eyes bulged out like frogs' eyes. "That can't be right!"

"I've checked it twice," said Lief.

"Let's run a different sample," she said, pulling up a chair. The two of them seemed to have forgotten completely about the girls.

"What's going on?" said Amy. "Why are you both so surprised?"

Lief must have finally remembered them. "I'm surprised because my screen says this fish is loaded with mercury," he said. "One part per million."

"Is that a lot?" asked Erin.

He nodded. "You bet. And it explains why the fish seemed so sluggish as I was collecting them."

"But where did the mercury come from?" asked Robin.

"I'm not sure," said Lief grimly. "I can tell you this, though. If there *is* mercury in these samples, the river is in big trouble."

Chapter Four

Lief and Susan spent the rest of the morning testing like crazy. While they tested, the girls asked them questions, like how the mercury got into the fish (it was probably discharged into the water, where it was absorbed into the plants and then eaten by the fish) and whether or not *people* should eat the fish (definitely not). They also learned that the level of mercury the fish were showing was above the EPA's (Environmental Protection Agency) acceptable level, which meant the river would have to be closed for fishing.

"How are you going to find the source of the contamination?" asked Erin, sounding like an employee of the Parks Department.

"Depends," said Lief, stroking his beard. "Maybe we can monitor the concentrations through the mussels."

"Huh?" said Robin.

"The Meramec has a large mussel population," he explained. "Since the mussels are stationary, we can randomly test groups of them and follow the contamination to its source."

"I get it," said Erin, who was the only one who did. "Mussels don't move like fish do, so the closer they are to the mercury, the more contamination they'll have."

"Right," said Lief. "Theoretically, we can trace the mercury upstream or downstream just by following the mussels."

"Wow," said Amy. "That's cool."

Lief grinned. "Even cooler if we can prove it."

"Can we come with you to get the mussels?" asked Erin.

Lief glanced at the clock. "Not today. I've got a softball game in thirty minutes."

"How about tomorrow?" said Amy.

Lief sighed. "Just my luck. My only day off and the river is suddenly teeming with mercury. Okay. I've got room for two of you in the boat."

"We'll go," said Amy and Erin in unison, leaving Robin and Leah looking relieved.

"Make sure you get your parents' permission," he said.

"We will," said Amy. "Wow. What a great story this'll make for the paper."

Lief's face clouded over. "Not a word until we figure out what's going on, okay? I don't want anyone jumping to conclusions. This could just be a fluke."

"Sure," said Amy.

"I mean it," said Lief. "We have to go about this very carefully. This isn't kids' play anymore."

Amy swallowed. "I know."

She felt his eyes slicing through her. "Good. As long as we're clear."

On their way home, the four of them talked about everything that had happened that day, trying to get it all to make sense. "Is mercury in the river *really* that big a deal?" asked Leah, walking along beside Erin's bike.

"It's poison!" said Robin. "Didn't you hear what Lief said?"

"But can it kill you?"

"If enough gets into your system I bet it can," said Amy.

"But I'm not planning to eat any fish from there," said Leah. "I only like filet of sole."

"But other people eat the fish," said Erin. "And so do animals like muskrats and raccoons. When something gets into the water that affects the fish, the balance of nature is upset in all directions."

"What's that supposed to mean?" asked Robin.

"It's like a big chain reaction," said Erin. "In nature, everything depends on something else. For example, if all the fish died, then there would be nothing left in the river to eat the plants."

"And if there were too many plants, the river would get choked up and eventually die out," said Amy.

Robin looked at her. "What are you? Erin's assistant?"

Amy blushed. "I just paid attention in science class, that's all." She stopped her bike. "Does anyone want to come back to the treehouse? I can make us all lunch."

"I'll have something," said Robin. "I'm starved."

"Me, too," said Erin. "As long as it's not fish."

"I can't come," said Leah, wrinkling her nose. "Celeste is taking me shopping."

"What's wrong with that?" asked Robin. Celeste was Leah's mother. She worked as a buyer for Saks Fifth Avenue, so clothes were important to her.

Leah groaned. "I guess you've never been shopping with Celeste, Robin." Leah was an artist, so naturally she had style, but it was nothing like Celeste's. Leah preferred black and trendy while Celeste liked matching combos. They drove each other crazy.

"I guess not," said Robin. "Maybe I should consider myself lucky."

No one was home when Amy, Robin, and Erin arrived fifteen minutes later. Amy dug through the freezer, looking for something to fix. "All right!" she said, tugging on a box in the back. "Microwave burritos!" She nuked them, then grabbed a few sodas from the fridge. "Okay. Let's go, guys."

The minute they hit the treehouse, Amy knew she was in trouble. "What's this mess doing in here?" asked Erin, climbing through the hatch. A couple of empty soda cans and a bag of pretzels lay on the floor. The sofa cushions were scattered around the room.

"And what's all this junk on the walls?" said Robin.

"It's Grant's weather station," said Amy. She cleared a space on her desk for the food, then picked up a dirty tissue and dropped it into the wastebasket.

"Doesn't he know about garbage cans?" demanded Erin.

"I guess not," said Amy. Darn! She'd *told* him to clean up.

"Look what he did to the Crow's Nest," said Robin, sticking her head up there. "It's got all sorts of weird stuff in it." She dropped back down to the floor. "You'd better say something to him, Amy. He's spread out all over the place and he's making a mess. We didn't give him permission to take over."

"Yeah," said Erin. "We had an agreement, remember? If he can't clean up after himself, he's out."

"What if I give him a warning?" said Amy.

"You'd better do something," said Erin. She took one of the cushions from the floor, tossed it back onto the sofa, and sat down. "Oh my gosh," she said. She leaned over to pull something out from between the other two cushions.

"What is it?" said Amy.

She dangled a small silver earring set with purple stones in the air. "Remember this?"

Robin gasped. "An earring like the one Elvis found! What's it doing here?"

"Good question," said Erin. "At least now we know where Elvis found the other one."

"Maybe Grant has a girlfriend," said Robin. Right after she said it, she looked at Amy. "Sorry."

"I don't care," said Amy quickly. She stared at the earring. Where had she seen that thing before? And what was Grant doing up here with a girl . . . she'd never seen him with a girl before. All he cared about were his inventions.

"Now I *know* you'd better say something to him," said Robin. "The treehouse isn't for dating."

"Or trashing," said Erin. She tilted her head. "Do you hear someone?" She leaned out the window to see who it was, then yelled, "What do you want? Go away!"

"Who is it?" asked Robin.

"Roddy. Now we have Roddy bothering us.

Beat it, Roddy! Grant's not up here!" She gave Amy a look like it was all her fault.

"Okay, okay," said Amy. "I'll talk to him."

"When?" said Robin.

"I don't know." Amy wished Erin hadn't found that stupid earring.

Erin cast her eye around the room and then took a long, slow bite out of her burrito. "I'd say the sooner the better, Amy. He has an agreement, remember?"

Amy spent the rest of the afternoon avoiding the treehouse and Grant. She knew she needed to talk to him, but she couldn't bring herself to do it. Maybe if she didn't think about it, the problem would solve itself.

The next morning, she and Erin went out on Lief's boat. Good thing Lief had given them his home phone number the day before, just in case their parents wanted to call and check him out, which of course they did. He'd passed their approval, though, and now the three of them were putting along the river in his little outboard.

"Whee," said Erin, putting out her arm to catch the wind. "Where to?"

"We'll work our way upstream first," he said. "I have a hunch I want to follow."

As they rode along, Lief talked about the river. "We refer to the Meramec in two portions, the upper and lower. For the most part, the upper Meramec is still in its natural vegetative state, while the lower portion, which runs through here, has been more affected by mankind."

"How?" said Amy.

Lief pointed to a large sandy gravel bar that had a couple of tractors parked on it. "Take that gravel mining operation," he said. "It has a direct effect on the mussel habitat."

"Why?" said Erin.

"Because freshwater mussels need flowing water to survive. As the tractors dig down forty or fifty feet into the stream to gather gravel, they turn the flowing, shallow water into deep, stagnant pools."

"Oh," said Erin.

They rode a while longer, through an area of warehouses and factories. Lief slowed the motor down to a sputter. "Let's pick up our first batch of mussels right here." He pulled a weird contraption out from under the bow. "This is a viewing box," he said. It looked sort of like a submarine periscope with a piece of glass attached to one end.

Lief stuck the end with the glass on it down into the water and peered into the other end of the tube. "This lets us look for mussels in the water without the glare of the sun to bother us." He moved the viewing box back and forth until he found what he wanted. "Here we go." He rolled up his sleeves and plunged his hand deep into the water. Seconds later, he pulled up a couple of crusty-looking mussels that reminded Amy of burnt oatmeal cookies.

"That's them?" said Amy.

"That's them." Lief stuck the mussels into a mesh collecting bag. "Let's get a few more here, then pick up some more back by the boat launch."

After they'd finished their collecting, they headed back to the lab. "Now do we do our tests?" said Erin.

"We'll run a few today and save the rest for tomorrow," said Lief. "I don't want to lose my *whole* day off."

He pried open the mussel shells and mushed up the meat the same way he had done with the fish, wrapping the extra mussels in tinfoil and throwing them into the freezer next to Chester.

"Do you think my muskrat has mercury in him?" asked Erin.

"Probably," said Lief. "The dangerous thing about mercury contamination is that it magnifies as it moves up the food chain. For example, every time a muskrat eats a contaminated fish or mussel, the mercury in that fish or mussel is absorbed by the muskrat." He reached in for Chester. "Want to find out?"

"No, not right now," said Erin quickly. You'd have thought Chester had been a pet of hers.

"I'll test him later," said Lief.

They ran the test twice, once for the mussels near the factories and once for the ones near the boat launch. "Bingo," said Lief.

"Were you right?" said Amy.

"Looks like it. The mercury contamination by the factories is significantly higher. Maybe one and a half parts per million."

"So does that mean the mercury is coming from one of the factories?" asked Erin.

"That's a reasonable guess," said Lief. "Someone is probably flushing it right into the water, along with their other wastes."

"Wow," said Amy. "That's against the law I bet."

"Sure is."

"So why would someone do that? Why would they deliberately put poison into the water?"

Lief's mouth set itself into a straight line. "Because disposing toxic waste is expensive and time-consuming, that's why. We have strict laws in this country stating how and where toxic wastes can be put. For some people, though, it's easier and cheaper just to dump the stuff illegally."

"That's terrible," said Amy.

"I know," said Lief.

Erin said, "What if we can find where the mercury is coming from? Can we have the people who are doing it arrested?"

He shook his head. "The punishment is usually a fine. And what's a few thousand dollars to a company that's making millions?"

"But we have to stop them," said Amy.

"Oh, we can do that much," said Lief. "We'll make as big a stink out of this as we can, don't worry about that. I tell you what. Tomorrow we'll go out again and do some looking around to see if we can find any pipes discharging sewage into the water."

Amy took her reporter's notebook out of

her back pocket. "Then we can write our story?"

"Not yet," said Lief. "Mercury mixed in with other chemicals is indistinguishable, so even if we think we've found where it's coming from, we still have to produce solid evidence."

Amy was starting to feel a little discouraged. "How do we do *that?*" she said in an exasperated voice.

Lief smiled patiently. "Don't worry," he said. "We have our ways. What time can you get here?"

Amy and Erin looked at each other. "I have soccer practice, but I can get out of it," said Erin. "Three-thirty?"

"Three-thirty it is," said Lief. "See you then."

Chapter Five

After Erin and Amy left Lief, they headed right for the treehouse. Erin thought it would be a good idea to go over everything that had happened so far, to make sure their notes were complete.

They parked their bikes by the garage and were on their way to the treehouse when they noticed Robin waving to them from the window. "Come on up," she said. "You won't believe it."

This time Amy was the first one through the hatch.

"He did it again," said Robin, before Amy even had a chance to say anything like "Oh no."

For the second time, the cushions were scattered on the floor, and empty soda cans and food wrappers dotted the room.

"What do you think?" said Erin, scrambling up behind her.

Amy sighed. "Maybe he's coming right back." Just then she noticed a pretty blond girl with dark eyes whom she'd never seen before, sitting quietly in the corner.

"This is Kelly Livingston," said Robin, introducing her. "She's the one who's going to do the movie review, remember? I told her not to move until you got here, so you could see the room *exactly* as we found it."

"Oh, hi," said Amy, still in a state of shock. Why was Grant doing this? He *knew* he was on probation for thirty days.

"Hi," said Kelly. "I love your newspaper. Robin's been showing me some of your old issues."

"Kelly came home with me from Sunday School today and I wanted you to meet her," said Robin. She threw out her arm. "So what do you think? Is Grant the biggest pig you've ever met?"

"Maybe you should have said something

to him yesterday,'' said Erin, making Amy feel even worse.

Amy stared at the hatch. It was true. She couldn't put off talking to Grant any longer. She had to say something to him right now.

Grant's mother seemed surprised to see someone other than Roddy ringing their front doorbell. ''Is Grant expecting you?'' she asked, looking confused. She had Grant's same moon face and bulky build.

''No,'' said Amy.

His mother glanced up the stairs. ''He hates to be interrupted when he's working on something.''

No wonder he was weird, thought Amy. His mother allowed it. ''Maybe if you tell him it's me and it's important,'' she said.

Mrs. Taylor hesitated. ''Okay. Why don't you go on up?''

Amy knocked as politely as she could on Grant's door. ''Hi, Grant. Are you there? It's me. Amy.''

She could hear Grant banging things around inside his den of invention.

''Can I come in? I need to talk to you.''

The door slowly opened. Amy screamed.

Grant's face was hidden behind a huge nozzle mask, and in his hand was a giant blowtorch.

He pulled the mask up. "What's the matter?"

"You look like some kind of alien ant," she said, shuddering. "What are you doing, anyway?"

"Fooling around."

He was lucky he hadn't blown up his room or the neighborhood. Spontaneous combustion could have a real party in Grant's room. He wandered over to his desk, if you could call it that, and pulled a piece of paper off it. "Here. It's my first weather prediction."

"Oh," she said, not bothering to take it. "Did you get it from the radio?"

Grant looked hurt. "No! I figured this one out. Didn't you see all the weather charts?"

"I guess." She looked around for evidence of a girlfriend . . . a picture, maybe a hair ribbon . . . but she didn't notice anything except Grant's usual junk. "Um, Grant . . . we're having a little problem with the treehouse."

"I knew it! I'm *not* the only one having trouble getting through that hatch, am I?"

"Not exactly."

His round face softened. "What, then?"

"Remember when we said that you could put your weather station up there, but that you were on thirty days' probation?"

"What about it?"

"You're about to lose it."

He seemed honestly surprised. "How come?"

"Because the last two times we were up there, it was a mess. Cushions on the floor, empty soda cans, dirty tissues." She skipped the earring.

"I didn't leave any cushions or food lying around," he said. "I cleaned up perfectly."

Amy looked at him suspiciously. "You did?"

"Scout's honor." He put his hand across his chest.

The guilt started to creep in. "Wait a second," said Amy. "Since when were you a Boy Scout?"

"I still mean the promise. Honest. I didn't make any mess." He pressed his weather forecast into her hand.

She wanted to believe him. She did believe him . . . almost. "Then if it's not you, who is it?"

"I don't know. I have no idea."

She gave him the evil eyeball. "Are you *sure?*"

"I swear," said Grant, who was starting to look mad.

It was the mad look that convinced her he was telling the truth. Now all she had to do was convince the others . . . or even better, find the guilty person before Grant got into any more trouble.

The next afternoon, when Amy and Erin arrived at the Parks Department shed, Lief was already waiting for them outside, dressed in his usual outdoorsman clothes. "Ready?" he said, starting down the path to the boat launch before they had a chance to reply.

As they hurried after him, he called over his shoulder, "I've already loaded up the boat. Try to be quick, please."

Amy and Erin silently did as they were told. Anyone could see that today he meant business. Once they were underway, though, Lief seemed to relax a little. "It's important that we go about this as inconspicuously as possible," he said, guiding the little boat along. "If anyone should see what we're up to, we wouldn't want that person removing the evidence, *comprende?*"

"*Sí,*" said Erin.

Lief smiled and shifted the blade of grass he was chewing on from one side of his mouth to the other. "Now, *what* we're looking for is some sort of sewer pipe, which will be discharging dirty-looking water into the river. It'll probably be somewhat hidden."

As they rounded the bend and reached the factory area, Lief slowed the boat down. "Okay. Here we are, folks. Keep your eyes peeled. Amy, you take the left bank, Erin, the right. If you see anyone watching you, just smile and wave, like you're out for an afternoon boat ride."

Amy twisted her head to the left and let her eyes skim the banks. The rusted front seat of a car sat half-buried in the sand, its back resting against a fallen tree trunk. This part of the river bank was thickly overgrown with vines and freshly sprouted weeds. How would they ever spot a little pipe in all this?

"Can you go any slower?" asked Erin, as if she were reading Amy's mind.

"I can try," said Lief. The boat suddenly whooshed forward. "Sorry. We hit a riffle."

"A what?" said Amy, not daring to turn her head.

"A stream current," said Lief. "The Meramec is a series of what we call pools and riffles . . . basically slow and fast parts. Don't worry if you don't see anything," he added. "We'll ride closer to the banks on our next go-round."

Amy was just starting to realize that this might be a two or three day operation when Erin suddenly called out, "Wait!"

Amy jerked her head to the right.

"What's that?" She pointed to a metal pipe poking out of the side of the bank.

"Don't know," said Lief, aiming the boat toward shore. "Let's find out."

As they got closer, they could see that the pipe was about eight inches across. Slimy brown liquid poured from its mouth and oozed down the bank into the stream.

"Can you see where it's coming from?" asked Lief.

Her eyes followed the pipe up the slope and over to a large industrial building set back from the river. "Lectro International," she read. "No trespassing."

"Figures," said Lief. "Lectro manufactures electric lights."

"Do light bulbs have mercury in them?" asked Erin.

"Fluorescent ones do," he said. Grabbing a tree branch, Lief pulled their boat up alongside the pipe. "Hand me that container, would you?" he said, pointing to a glass test tube on the bottom of the boat. He put on some thick gloves and then took the test tube and stuck it directly underneath the oozing gunk.

"Now do we go test it?" said Amy.

Lief capped the test tube with a rubber plug. "Not this stuff," he said. "This gets sent out to another lab."

"How soon do we get the results?" asked Amy.

"Couple of days," said Lief. He pushed the boat away from the shore and started up the engine. "You two in a hurry?"

Amy glanced at Erin. "No," she said. "As long as we're back before dark."

"Good," said Lief. "Just to be safe, I want to keep looking. You never know what else you'll find when you start poking around."

* * *

Luckily or unluckily, they didn't find any more pipes or suspicious leaks before dark. The next afternoon was the regular staff meeting of the newspaper, though, and you could bet Amy and Erin would have a lot to talk about.

That afternoon, Amy arrived early to make sure the place was clean, which it was, thank goodness. As soon as everyone was seated, Amy opened the meeting by filling in Leah and Robin on their adventure with Lief.

"Wow," said Robin, after Amy told the story. "What a scoop."

"Yeah," said Erin. "Wait until the real paper sees what we found this time. I hope Lectro gets a huge fine."

"This issue comes out a week from Friday," said Amy, pulling out her notebook and tapping her glasses with her forefinger. "What do we have so far?" Then she added, "Besides our lead story?"

"We have my pictures and Robin's story from the river clean-up," said Leah.

"And Kelly's movie review," said Robin. "She's going to see her movie this weekend."

"What's she seeing?" asked Erin.

"She's not sure yet."

"What about Grant?" said Erin.

The room got quiet. "Oh," said Amy, reaching into her bookbag. "Here's his weather prediction for this week. Let's see if he's right. Today was supposed to be cloudy in the morning and then clearing. Wow! He was right!"

"What about the mess?" asked Leah.

"Yeah," said Robin. "Don't tell us the weather. Did he confess?"

Amy looked at her friends. "He didn't do it, guys."

"Get out of here," said Robin. "Who else would have done it?"

"I don't know," she said. "But he swears he didn't make the mess and I believe him."

"Then what about this equipment all over the place?" said Erin.

"He needs it for his predictions," said Amy. She glanced around the room. "You know what? None of us has even bothered to ask him how it all works."

"Who cares?" said Robin, bursting into a big laugh.

Amy's fists tightened. "I do."

Robin stopped smiling.

"We promised to give him a thirty-day trial, and that's what he's going to get, okay?" In a tight voice she added, "Any more business for today?"

"We haven't talked much about the rest of the issue," said Erin in a teeny voice.

"What about it?" barked Amy.

Erin's eyes popped open wide.

"Sorry," said Amy. "I didn't mean to yell at you." Why was she so upset? It wasn't Erin's fault. "Weren't you working on a list of ways people could help save the planet?"

Erin held up her list. "Put a weighted plastic bottle in the toilet, recycle old cans and newspapers, shut off lights and water when you're not using them, don't use Styrofoam cups, ask for paper bags at the grocery store and then re-use them . . ."

"Do *you* do all this?" interrupted Leah.

"Of course," said Erin. "We even have a compost pile."

"Haven't you ever seen it?" said Robin. "It's disgusting. All this fruit and grass rotting together in a big wire basket in their backyard."

"No one's asking you to be that committed, Robin," said Erin.

"Guys, guys," said Leah. "Stop it."

"The peacemaker speaks," said Robin.

"Wait," said Amy, trying to stop things

before they got any more out of control. "This Earth Day issue is important. I don't think we should criticize each other."

"Fair enough," said Erin, backing down.

Amy kept expecting to hear from Lief, but the next few days went by without a word from him. At home, Amy concentrated on finishing the rest of the issue, while at school she spent her time avoiding Grant.

Friday afternoon, Amy was on her way to science when Robin sidled up to her in the hallway. "Did you see who Danielle Stevens was talking to all the way through lunch?"

"No," said Amy.

"Grant," said Robin.

Amy shrugged. "So?"

"That's not the first time, either. She's been talking to him a *lot* lately."

"I never noticed that," said Amy. She looked up and gulped. At that moment Grant was walking past with Danielle right beside him. Talk about timing!

"Hi, Robin. Hi, Amy," said Danielle, interrupting her conversations about constellations to give them a smile.

"Hi," said Amy, not very cheerfully. Since

when was Danielle interested in constellations?

They breezed on by.

"Did you see?" said Robin.

"See what?"

"She had on earrings," said Robin. "Long, dangly earrings."

"So?"

Robin leaned in closer. "Amy! What did we find in the treehouse the other day?" Before Amy could answer Robin said, "We found an earring, remember? A long, dangly earring. Now. What do you want to bet Grant has been entertaining visitors in *our* treehouse?"

"Impossible," said Amy, staring nervously down the hall. "I think I would have remembered if I'd seen those earrings on Danielle."

"I'll prove it," said Robin.

Amy's stomach curled into a little ball. "You will? How?"

"Easy. I'll just show Danielle the earrings and ask if they're hers. *Then* we'll know without any doubt who's telling the truth around here and who's lying."

Amy glanced down the hall where she noticed Grant starting to walk away from Danielle's locker. "See you later," Danielle was calling after him. "Same time, same place."

Grant, the skunk, cheerfully nodded his head up and down as he continued on to his next class.

Chapter Six

"NOTICE. STAY OUT! THIS TREEHOUSE OFF-LIMITS EXCEPT TO ERIN, LEAH, ROBIN, AND AMY. THIS MEANS YOU!" Amy underlined the YOU and then picked up the sign and carried it over to the far wall, where she hammered it in so well it would probably stick there forever. When she was finished she tossed the hammer harder than she should have onto the sofa, where she pictured Danielle and Grant discussing cloud formations.

"Amy. Are you up there?"

"Oh, hi Robin," said Amy, bringing herself back to reality. "What are you doing here?" She paused. "Did you ask Danielle about the earrings?"

"Not yet," said Robin, pulling herself into the room. "I went by her house but she wasn't home." She noticed Amy's new sign.

"Like it?" said Amy.

"Has Grant seen it?"

She shook her head. "Not yet. I was hoping you'd been to Danielle's." Deep down, she was still trying to give Grant the benefit of the doubt.

"Don't worry. I'll get there," said Robin. She waved an envelope at Amy. "I have Kelly's movie review."

"Great!" said Amy, taking the envelope and opening it. At least the movie review was done and out of the way. "The movie I want to tell you about is *Breathless*," she read. "It is a story of love and passion." Amy gave a gasp which came out sounding like a squawk. "She went to see *Breathless?* That has an R rating!"

"So?"

"So people under seventeen aren't admitted without an adult," said Amy. "How did she get in? I thought her dad was a minister."

"Just read the review, would you?" said Robin.

Amy read on. "The main character, Jacques, loves women. First he meets a woman named Francoise and then . . ." Her eyes skimmed the next line. "She can't write that!" she said, blushing. "This is a family newspaper."

Robin giggled.

Maybe this was Kelly's idea of a joke? Amy read the rest of the review. It got pretty detailed. "She's not serious, is she?"

"Why not?" said Robin.

"Because," said Amy. "We can't review an R-rated movie."

"It's a free country," said Robin.

"But a lot of our readers are kids."

"And a lot are grown-ups," said Robin.

Amy handed the review back to Robin. "Sorry. Tell her to do something else."

"She's not going to like it."

Amy sighed. "Just tell her we can't accept it, okay?"

"Okay," said Robin. "But I'm warning you. You may be asking for it."

When Amy got back to the house she found a note from Patrick. "Call Leaf," it said.

She hurried to Patrick's room, where she

found him lying on his bed listening to his headphones.

"When did Lief call?" she yelled, loud enough for him to hear.

"I don't know," he said. "A while ago." His head bobbed up and down.

"Did he leave a phone number?"

Bob, bob, bob. "I couldn't find a pencil."

"Great," said Amy, throwing up her arms. She hurried into her parents' bedroom and dragged the phone book out from under the bed, along with about sixteen dust balls. "Now where is the Parks Department?" she said aloud. She ran her finger along the page.

It took about five phone calls to track down the right number. "Hi, Lief," she said, when she finally reached him. "It's Amy Evans." She always included her last name when speaking to grown-ups.

"Oh hi," said Lief. "I got the lab results in. I think we've found our source."

"Great!" said Amy.

"Do you have a pencil?" said Lief.

Amy grabbed the message pad off her parents' night table. What a scoop!

"Here's what I want you to write . . ."

"I know what to write," Amy interrupted.

Lief must not have heard her. "Dangerous

amounts of mercury contamination have recently been discovered in fish in the Meramec River," he said. "The contamination has been traced to Lectro International, a large manufacturing company situated on the river. Contamination levels in fish and mussels ranged from three and a half to four parts per million, well above the EPA's acceptable range."

"Wait a second," said Amy, writing as fast as she could. "What was that last part?"

"Contamination levels ranged from three and a half to four parts per million," he repeated.

Amy wrote down the figure and frowned. Something wasn't right.

"I'm sure you can fill in the rest of the facts," Lief was saying. "Your paper comes out next Saturday, right?"

"Right," said Amy.

"Then I'm going to call the *Post-Dispatch* on Thursday, so their story breaks at about the same time."

Amy suddenly remembered what Lief said that was bothering her. "It was one part per million," she said aloud.

"Pardon?"

"Didn't you tell us the concentration level was one to one and a half parts per million?"

"No," said Lief. "Three and a half to four."

"Are you sure?"

"Positive. I'll show you my figures. Anything else?"

"Um, I guess not." Confused, she hung up the phone. She sat for a few minutes, thinking, then picked up the phone and dialed Erin's number. "Guess what?" she said when Erin answered.

"What?"

"Lief called. He said the mercury was coming from the pipe you found."

"Wow. Now what?"

"Now I guess we write our story." She paused. "You wouldn't happen to remember the contamination level, would you?"

"That 'parts' thing?" said Erin. "Sure. It was one part per million in the fish and one and a half parts per million in the mussels. Why?"

Amy tapped her glasses with her finger. "Lief swears it was three and half to four parts per million."

"Why would he say that?"

"I'm not sure," said Amy. "Is there a big difference between one and four?"

"I don't know," said Erin. "I can ask Dad."

"Would you?"

"Sure. I'll call you later, okay?"

"That would be great," said Amy. She stretched out on her parents' bed and stared, distracted, at a spider slowly heading for the light fixture. She moved her knees back and forth restlessly. Down the hall, Patrick had begun singing along with his headphones. "Oh, baby, baby." His voice wobbled back and forth like a kindergartner's.

The doorbell rang. "I'll get it," said Amy, glad for an excuse to be doing something other than watching a spider or listening to Patrick's solo concert. She ran downstairs and threw open the door. "Oh. It's you."

Grant stood looking like a giant drowned rat. His brown hair was plastered to his head and perspiration clung to his shirt, exposing his chest muscles. Amy waited for his confession. "Do you have a cup of water I can borrow?"

"A what?" She couldn't believe it. Where was his apology? His remorse?

"My hygrometer isn't working correctly."

Amy's eyes narrowed. "Didn't you see my sign?"

Grant gave her a dumb look. "What sign?"

"In the treehouse. It says everyone except newspaper staff is supposed to keep out."

He wiped his face with the back of his arm. "Why? Are you having a meeting?"

"Grant! Do I have to explain everything to you?"

He still didn't get it.

"Your thirty-day trial is over early," she said in her iciest voice. "Find somewhere else for your weather station."

Grant gave his wounded giant look. "But I haven't done anything wrong."

"Oh yeah?" said Amy. "That's not what I hear." She started to close the door on his size eleven sneakers.

"No fair!" yelled Grant, jamming his toe in the crack. "I'm being blamed for something I didn't do. Honest."

"Sorry," said Amy. Using all her strength, she managed to squeeze his foot out, then slam her body against the door.

There was silence, then a big voice sounding small said, "I thought you believed me."

Amy stared at the spot where Grant's toe had just been. "So did I," she said softly.

"Amy, aren't you going to have any dinner?"

Amy looked down at the huge portion of chili rellenos her mother had dished up for her fifteen minutes earlier. "I'm not that hungry, Mom."

"But this is your favorite," she said.

"That's right," added Patrick with a leering grin. "And not only that, it's probably the only time Mom is going to cook for us this entire week."

"Patrick! That's enough!" said Amy's father.

"Are you *sure* nobody called for me when I was out in the treehouse before dinner?" asked Amy. "Robin or Erin or . . ." She wanted to say Grant, but instead she said, "anybody?"

"Positive," said her mother. "I was standing here beside the phone the entire time I was cooking."

Patrick folded his hands. "You see, Amy. Chili rellenos is a very complex dish."

"Patrick!" said Amy's father, slamming his hand on the table. "I've had enough of your sarcasm."

"Amy, honey," said her mother. "Instead of waiting for your calls, why don't you call *them?*"

"I guess I could." She slid her chair out. "May I be excused?"

She called Robin first, but no one was home. Erin's family was in the middle of dinner. "I can only talk a minute," she told Amy. "What's up?"

"Did you ask your dad about the parts?"

"He's not here," she said. "I forgot he had a seminar in Columbia for two days. He won't be back until tomorrow night."

Amy groaned. "Great. More bad news."

"Why? What else is bad?"

Amy didn't say anything.

"Is something else the matter?"

"I don't feel like talking about it," she said. She could hear Erin's mother in the background calling Erin back to the table. "You'd better go."

"Okay," said Erin. "But don't let whatever it is that's bothering you get you down."

"Yep," said Amy. "Bye."

That evening Amy went to bed early, mostly because she wanted to finish the book she was reading and a tiny bit because she didn't want to think about anything else. Amy loved to read in bed. She had a whole routine worked out. On her left side, she'd prop up a snack, like a bag of potato chips or a package of Ring Dings, and next to that would be her bike canteen filled with soda. If she set her book on her lap, then her right hand could turn the pages, preventing them from getting ruined by potato chip grease.

Amy stole two pillows from her parents' bedroom and settled in. Her parents were at a party at the Harrises' house and Patrick was *out*, so she had the whole house to herself.

She read for a long time, until she started feeling sleepy, at which point she got up and went into the bathroom to brush her teeth and get ready for bed. That's when she noticed the light coming from the treehouse.

She stared out the window. Only one person would be crazy enough to be in the treehouse right now. Grant!

Amy drummed her fingers against the windowpane. What was he doing in there? He wouldn't dare be up there with Danielle, would he?

She quickly ran to her room and got dressed. Seconds later, she quietly slipped out the kitchen door, determined to find out.

She hadn't taken more than two steps across the lawn when she heard giggles floating down from the tree.

Amy stopped. Giggles??? After their conversation? After the sign she'd so carefully nailed up? Boy! Did he have nerve! She stalked the rest of the way across the lawn and started noisily up the ladder. That should give them plenty of warning.

"What do you guys think you're doing in here?" she announced, flinging open the hatch. She just about choked when she saw Patrick and Heather Hartford sitting straight up on the sofa like a couple of bowling pins. "Patrick! What are *you* doing in here?"

"Talking," said Patrick. "What does it look like?"

"Hi, Amy," said Heather, trying to sound casual.

Suddenly everything made sense.

"*Now* I remember!" said Amy. "Those were *your* earrings we found, weren't they, Heather?" Amy looked around the room. "And *you're* the ones who've been leaving this place a mess, aren't you?"

"What are you talking about?" said Patrick.

Amy pointed to the sign. "Can't you read? No trespassing!"

Patrick laughed. "We're not doing anything wrong. Besides, nobody else is using it right now."

"Maybe not," said Amy, stalking over to her desk and grabbing a pen. "But . . ." She marched over to her sign and added Grant's name in big, capital letters. "Sometimes Grant likes to work at night." She underlined his name with a flourish. "*And,* unlike you, Patrick, he happens to clean up after himself!"

As Amy headed back for the house she felt strangely satisfied. So it wasn't Grant and Danielle after all. She stared out at the treehouse uneasily. Still . . . if it wasn't them, then what had Danielle meant by "same time, same place?" The only way to get to the bottom of *that* was to ask Grant, first thing tomorrow morning.

Chapter Seven

The next morning, Amy put on her nicest jeans and her favorite sweater (the blue one with the pink flowers across the top), and then pulled her hair into a ponytail on top of her head. When she was finished, she took a long look at herself in the full-length mirror in her parents' bedroom. If only she could get rid of her glasses! Last year she'd begged her mother for contact lenses, but her mother had said she wasn't quite old enough. Maybe she'd bring it up again now that she was nearly finished with seventh grade.

She hurried down to the kitchen, where her parents were dressed in their Saturday clothes, reading the morning paper and drinking their coffee. "Hi, guys. I'm going over to Grant's, okay?"

Her father looked up from the sports section. "Grant Taylor's?"

"Yeah," said Amy, shooting out the door before they could wonder about anything else.

This time Mrs. Taylor didn't seem as surprised to see her. "Hello Amy," she said in a pleasant Mom voice. "Are you looking for Grant?"

"Is he here?"

"I think he's out back," she said. "He said something about moving his weather station out there."

"Thanks," she said, making a beeline for the backyard.

As Amy rounded the corner she saw Grant bent over a large wooden crate, which he seemed to be taking apart. Luckily he didn't notice her before her cheeks flared red and she had to go back and wait around the corner until they returned to normal. When they finally calmed down, she tried again.

"Hi."

Grant didn't even look up. "What do you

want?'' He pried off another board and tossed it onto the grass.

''Nothing.'' As soon as she said it, she wanted to kick herself. That was so dumb! Why did she say ''nothing''? ''I mean, I want to apologize. It wasn't you making the mess. It was Patrick. He's been going up there to make out with Heather Hartford.'' Thinking about making out made her face turn red all over again, and then *of course* that's when Grant decided to look at her.

''He was?''

She took a deep breath, hoping that would make the redness in her face go away faster. ''I'm really sorry I didn't believe you.''

''That's okay.''

She stared at the ground. ''And you don't have to move the weather station.''

''I don't?''

''Not if you don't want to.'' Grant seemed pleased. Amy put her hands in her pockets, then took them out and wrapped them around her body, then put them back in her pockets again.

Grant stopped what he was doing and looked her dead in the eye. ''How come you're so nervous?''

Her hands flapped out of control. "Me? Nervous?"

"Yeah. Why are your hands flapping around?"

She jammed them into her pockets. "They're fine. I'm just glad we worked things out." She took another deep breath. "What did Danielle mean yesterday when she told you, 'See you later'?"

Grant scowled. "Aw, nothing. We belong to this Wednesday night youth group at our church, that's all."

Amy stared.

"It was my mother's idea," said Grant. "She thought a group activity would be good for me."

There was a *long* silence and then Grant said, "I don't mind it that much, actually. Most of the time we just sit around listening to music."

Another, even longer silence followed, during which Amy tried desperately to think of something to say, something other than "sorry," which would sound so dumb. Finally she blurted, "Do you need any help with your weather station?"

"Oh," said Grant. "Yeah. I guess. Want me to show you how it works?"

"Sure," said Amy. They headed back over to her yard and up into the treehouse.

"It's actually pretty simple," said Grant, zeroing in on the wall chart. "See . . . you have this chart here . . ."

Amy moved closer to see.

"And each day you have to carefully record all this data . . . temperature, wind speed and direction, cloud cover, humidity. . . ." His arm brushed against hers, causing her cheeks to turn red again.

Suddenly, Grant bent over and kissed her on the lips.

"Grant!"

He grinned. Amy kissed him back. He grinned again. "I guess you're not mad at me anymore," he said.

"I guess not," she said, smiling. What a way to start the day.

As if there weren't enough excitement in Amy's life, Erin called that afternoon to tell her that she'd spoken with her father. "He said the difference between one part and four parts is a lot," she told Amy, who had already decided not to mention to her what had happened with Grant . . . yet. "If the river has four parts per million, it's enough to have the river closed down completely,'' said Erin. ''No one will be allowed near it, and Dad said the public is going to panic.''

''Wow,'' said Amy. ''That's bad. Do you think when Lief tested the other fish he found the higher levels in them?''

''Could be,'' said Erin. ''Dad said that the fish species highest in the food chain, like bass and walleye, absorb the most mercury. Maybe we should go talk to Lief in person.''

''I bet he's over there right now,'' said Amy.

''He's always over there,'' said Erin. ''I'll meet you in front of your house in ten minutes.''

As Amy and Erin rode up to the shed, they could see Lief sitting on the front steps, cleaning some sort of engine with an old rag. ''Look who's here!'' he said with a smile.

Amy leaned her bike against the shed and walked over to where Lief was working. ''What's that for?'' she asked, pointing to the engine.

''Belongs to the boat,'' he said. ''Did you get your story written?''

Amy glanced at Erin. ''Not yet.''

''Why not?''

"Um, because we were wondering about something," said Erin. "What did you say the contamination in the catfish was?"

"About four parts per million."

"What about the bass and walleye?" said Amy.

Lief pressed his lips together. "Slightly higher." He jammed the rag around the greasy engine parts. "Why?"

Erin said, "Because we both remember that you said the mercury contamination was one to one and a half parts per million."

Lief didn't say anything.

"Erin's father said there's a big difference between one and four, and we don't understand how the figure could have changed that much," said Amy.

Lief pushed the rag into one of the pipes and twisted it back and forth. Finally he said, "I should have known you guys would be quick enough to pick up on that."

"You mean you *did* change the figures?" said Amy. "Why?"

"Listen," he said. "Lectro International is a multi-million-dollar mega-corporation, reaping millions of dollars in profits every year . . . frequently at the expense of the environment. Do you think they care about a puny little fine?"

"But that's lying!" said Amy.

Erin said, "Wait. I don't understand. If you make the figures higher, does Lectro have to pay more?"

"Maybe," said Lief. "But money isn't my real motive." He threw down his rag. "Look. You want to *really* know why I'm doing this? Because the bottom line is that I care about what happens to this river. If I inflate the damage, make it look worse than it is, then maybe people will take more notice. Maybe it will cause enough panic to make people say, 'Hmm, those guys at Lectro are doing bad things. Maybe we shouldn't buy Lectro products anymore, or maybe we should get together and monitor these guys better.' What they're doing is serious. Maybe Lectro needs to be accountable to somebody. Maybe we all need to be more accountable to the earth."

Amy's head spun. Lief had a point, but she still couldn't believe he would try to use them like this. "Won't you get caught?" she said.

"Eventually."

"What will happen to you? Will you go to jail?"

He laughed. "The EPA will come in, do its own testing, and then issue a statement saying the original figures were inaccurate. By then, though, I'm hoping it'll be too late, that the damage to Lectro's reputation will already have been accomplished."

"You planned this whole thing!"

"What's wrong with that?" he said. "Don't you think Lectro planned to dump that mercury in the river and save themselves a few bucks? What's wrong with fighting back?"

"Nothing," said Amy. "I guess."

Lief stood up. "Well, I've got to get some work done around here."

"Wait," said Amy, who was still trying to piece everything together. "Does anyone else know what the right figures are?"

He lifted up the engine and headed toward the back of the shed. "No. Just you."

Amy looked at Erin. "I was afraid of that," she told her. "It has to be our decision whether to print them the right way or the wrong way."

"What do we do?" said Erin. "I want to help Lief but I don't want to lie to our readers."

Amy thought for a minute. "I know what you mean. I think it's time for Vicky."

The first year the newspaper had started, the girls had asked their neighbor and friend, Vicky Lamb, to act as their advisor. Vicky was a reporter for the real paper, the *St. Louis Post-Dispatch,* and she was always great at helping them figure out problems they might be having.

Now when Amy and Erin rode up to Vicky's house they noticed her right away, bent over the front bushes planting flowers. Vicky lived alone with her three cats: Horace, Wendell, and Wilkie. She always said they were like her children.

"Hi Vicky," Amy called out.

"Oh, hi," she said, straightening up. She was wearing her bathing suit top with some baggy shorts.

"Not working today, huh?" said Amy.

"Not yet," she said. Real reporters had to be ready to go at a moment's notice. Vicky had once told them that the reason she wasn't married was because she was married to her job.

Vicky waved her gardening shovel in the air. "I thought I'd get a jump on my tan and my garden this year, but I just heard on the radio that it's going to get cold again tonight." She brushed a strand of her fuzzy brown hair off her face. "What's up?" She looked from Amy to Erin.

Slowly and carefully, Amy explained the whole story, starting from the beginning. Every once in a while, Erin would add something or make a correction, which Amy didn't mind. If there was one thing Vicky insisted on, it was getting the facts straight.

When Amy was finished, Vicky sat down on the front steps of her house to think. "Interesting," she said finally. "What you're asking is, is it okay to alter the news if you think it serves some higher good?" Her cat Wendell came over and wove himself back and forth between her legs. "A famous reporter named Walter Lippman once said that a journalist should think of himself as a fly on the wall who sees all and feels nothing."

"But that's impossible," said Amy.

Vicky smiled. "I suppose it is," she said. "Our point of view is always colored somewhat by the way we've been brought up to think and feel." She paused. "Certainly in this case you have options."

"Like what?"

"Well, you can always attribute those figures directly, which is one way to take the sweat off you."

Erin said, "You mean when we write our story we say, '*According to Lief Hopper*, the contamination levels ranged from three and a half to four parts per million.' "

"Something like that," said Vicky.

"I get it!" said Amy. "We're only quoting him, not giving our own information." She stopped. "But as reporters, aren't we supposed to tell our readers everything we know?"

"It doesn't seem very honest," agreed Erin, "keeping something from our readers."

Vicky nodded. "It's true. You *are* keeping something. And maybe that's asking too much of yourselves. It's your call, though, guys." Amy sighed, and Vicky went on. "Maybe what you need to do before you make a decision is weigh all the pros and cons. What happens to the river if you print the information the right way? What happens if you print it the way Lief wants it?"

"If we make it sound as bad as Lief wants us to, a lot more people will notice," said

Erin. Wendell climbed into Vicky's lap and started purring like an engine.

Amy frowned.

"What is it, Amy?" said Vicky.

Amy reached over to give Wendell a scratch behind the ears. "I don't like this."

"Why not?"

"I see why Lief did what he did, but I guess it makes me mad that he put us in this position. I think maybe he thought he could take advantage of us because we were kids."

"Maybe you should say something to him," said Vicky. "Sometimes grown-ups forget that kids don't like to be put in awkward positions any more than adults do."

Amy stared at her. "What are *you* going to say in *your* paper, now that you know the figures aren't right?"

"Good question," said Vicky. "For one thing, I probably won't be assigned the story, since I'm busy with something else. That's still no excuse for pretending ignorance, though. I guess I'll have to ask myself the same questions you're asking yourselves."

Inside Vicky's house, the phone started ringing. "Uh-oh. What do you want to bet that's the office?" She brushed Wendell off her lap and hurried away to answer it. "Will you let me see the paper before it goes to press? I'm anxious to see what you decide." The screen door swung open and shut with a bang.

There was a moment of quiet. "Saved by the bell," said Erin.

Amy stared at the door. "You know something, Erin? I don't think she wants to think about this any more than we do." Wendell started looking for another lap to sit on. "Come on," said Amy, lifting him off her legs.

"Where are we going?"

"To the treehouse," she said. "We've got some decisions to make."

Chapter Eight

As Amy and Erin turned the corner on their bikes, they could see a group of kids walking up and down in front of Amy's house, chanting and carrying large signs.

"What's going on?" said Erin.

"Beats me," said Amy, pedaling faster. As she got closer, she recognized Kelly Livingston, leading the group in a chant. "Unfair, unfair." Amy quickly read some of the signs: "STOP CENSORSHIP;" "IT'S A FREE COUNTRY."

She slowed her bike down and noticed Robin sitting on the edge of the lawn, nervously consuming caramel chewies.

"What's going on here?" she said, pulling up and motioning to the crowd.

Robin added another caramel chewie to her load. "I told you you'd be sorry if you told Kelly no."

"But I don't understand," said Amy. "Where did all these kids come from?"

"She got practically the whole Sunday School to show up," said Robin glumly. "Everyone except the junior choir. *They're* coming after practice." They both watched as a car drove slowly past. "Watch the road, lady, will you?" Robin shouted to the driver.

Amy winced. "Is Kelly always this . . . extreme?"

"Don't get her started on animal rights," said Robin.

Kelly put down her sign and marched over to where Amy and Robin were sitting. "Why don't you like my review?" she demanded.

"It's not that I don't like it," said Amy. "I don't think it's right for our paper."

Erin, who by now had parked her bike beside Amy's and joined them, interrupted. "What's going on here?"

"Amy canned Kelly's review," said Robin.

"It was an R-rated movie!" said Amy. "Give me a break!"

"Which one?" said Erin.

"Breathless," said Kelly. "It was great."

Erin lifted her eyebrows. "Your parents let you see *Breathless?"*

Kelly shook her head. "No way. Hilary Ryan took us. It was Robin's idea."

"Robin!" said Amy.

Robin's face turned red from the bottom up. "Thanks a lot, Kelly." She shrugged and looked at Amy. "How was *I* supposed to know she would pick this one to review?"

"You aren't supposed to be at R movies anyway," said Amy.

Robin unwrapped a few more candies. "I was with an adult. Hilary turned seventeen last month, remember?"

"So you should have said something to Kelly once you found out what she was planning to write about," said Erin, rushing to Amy's defense.

"I didn't know until she gave it to me in Sunday School," said Robin. "Honest."

"I don't think it's fair of you to censor me," said Kelly. "Your newspaper gets read by a lot of adults, and they go to R movies all the time."

"I'm not censoring you," said Amy. "We

asked you to write something for us and we have the right to turn it down."

"But the only reason you're turning it down is because you don't approve of the subject matter," said Kelly. "That's censorship." She waved her sign at the other kids, signaling them to start up the chanting again.

"Hold it," said Amy. "Hold everything."

The noise got even louder.

Erin covered her ears. "Oh, brother." She turned to Robin. "See what you started?"

"Don't blame me! It was Amy's idea to have another reviewer." She stared down the street. "Uh-oh! What did I tell you? Here comes the junior choir."

The choir was being led purposefully along by a shorter, freckled version of Kelly. "That's Samantha, Kelly's sister," said Robin. Samantha had them all singing "This is My Country."

"What are we going to do?" said Erin. "How do we get them to stop?"

The two groups met and fused, spreading themselves even farther up and down the street. By now a crowd had started to gather on the opposite sidewalk and traffic was beginning to back up.

"This is so embarrassing," said Erin. "Is the review really that bad?"

Amy blushed. "Erin, if you think this is embarrassing, you should read the review."

Erin twisted her hands. "Well, we can't let these guys stay here . . . can we?"

Amy sighed. "They have their rights."

"Are you saying we should *ignore* this?"

Amy thought fast. "No . . . I'm saying we should retreat . . . to the treehouse. With all this noise, I can't think straight."

It was Erin's idea to call Leah on their way to the backyard. Between what had happened with Lief and now Kelly, some important decisions were going to have to be made. "Now is as good a time as any," Erin had said.

Luckily, the treehouse was unoccupied when Amy, Robin, and Erin got there. Amy didn't know what would have made her more embarrassed—finding Grant or finding Patrick and Heather. She still hadn't said anything to anyone about what had gone on earlier, but as soon as she was standing in the treehouse again, she started getting that funny feeling in her stomach that she'd felt when Grant kissed her.

"Hey!" said Erin. "Where did that KEEP OUT sign come from? And why is Grant's name scribbled in?"

That's all it took for Amy's cheeks to start their transformation. "Um, I can explain . . ."

But before she had a chance, Robin said, "By the way, you're safe, Amy. Those weren't Danielle's earrings."

"I know."

"You do?"

"They belonged to Heather Hartford." Amy quickly explained the whole story, finishing with, "And so it wasn't Grant after all. . . ."

"I knew it," said Robin. "Grant likes you, not Danielle."

"What makes you say that?" said Amy, feeling her cheeks take off again.

"I can just tell," said Robin.

Amy heard someone start up the ladder. "Leah?" she called nervously. "Is that you?"

"Yep," said Leah. She stuck her head inside the room. "What's going on in front of your house?" She stared at Amy. "And why is your face all red?"

Amy fanned it with her hand. "It must be

warm up here.'' She quickly filled Leah in on the protesters.

"May I see the review?'' she asked.

"Me, too,'' said Erin.

"Sure,'' said Amy. She dug it out of her folder and handed it to Leah, who sat down next to Erin to read it.

As they read, every few seconds Erin would say, "Oh'' or "Wow.''

"Well?'' said Robin when they finished. "Should we or shouldn't we?''

"It's not exactly for kids,'' said Erin.

"I thought it was tasteful, though,'' said Leah.

"Figures,'' said Erin.

Leah gave her a dirty look. "I don't see anything wrong with publishing it. The rest of our paper has news for adults . . . why shouldn't the movie review be for adults?''

"But the subject matter isn't appropriate for kids,'' said Amy.

"We're not saying they should go to the movie,'' said Leah. "They can't get in anyway—unless they're a friend of Hilary's.''

"She has a point,'' said Robin. "Besides, it's not like kids won't know what she's writing about. They put sex and violence on TV all the time. Look at the soap operas.'' All of them except Amy faithfully watched the soap *Loving and Living.*

Amy thought about everything that had been said. Maybe they were right. Who was she trying to protect? Just because *she* didn't like the subject matter, did that give her the right to stop it from being published? She looked around at the others. "Okay. I'm willing to print the review as long as we don't make a habit out of reviewing R movies. Guys?"

"Sounds good to me," said Erin.

"Me, too," said Leah.

"Besides," she added with a grin, "I hate the idea of anyone accusing a newspaper of censorship."

"Good," said Robin, slipping off the sofa. "Then if nobody minds, I'll go tell Kelly she can take her Sunday School home."

Once the issue of the movie review had been settled, there was only the problem of Lief. In her heart, Amy knew it was wrong to lie, but in her head, she knew it was important to protect the river.

"So what's happening with the mercury story?" asked Robin almost on cue when she got back.

Amy and Erin looked at each other. "The river's in big trouble," said Erin. "Lectro International is illegally dumping mercury."

"Wow," said Robin. "Is it a lot?"

Erin glanced at Amy and then said firmly, "Lief said three and a half to four parts per million. Enough to close the river to everyone."

Amy's stomach turned two giant flips but she didn't say anything to correct Erin. She waited to see if Robin or Leah would catch the different figure.

Robin gave them both a satisfied smile. "That's great. I love it when we do some good."

Amy let out her breath.

"How long will it take for the river to be clean again?" asked Leah, doodling on her sketch pad.

Erin glanced sideways at Amy. "It depends. Once the mercury gets into the food chain, its effect is felt for a long time."

"Thank you, Professor Valdez," said Robin. "What does Lectro say?"

Amy stopped.

Robin stared at her. "You mean you didn't talk to them? You? Ms. Perfect?"

"She meant to," said Erin. "Right?"

Amy nodded, still thinking about what they'd just done. "I guess I was so busy getting the other side of the story, I forgot. I'll call them right now, okay?"

Robin said, "Watch out. If they're guilty they won't return your phone calls. That's what happens on *60 Minutes.*"

Amy smiled faintly.

"Is something wrong?" asked Leah.

"No," said Amy. "I hope not."

Robin was right about Lectro. Although Amy tried reaching several people, even telling them why she was calling, no one ever returned a phone call.

By Wednesday afternoon the issue was in good enough shape that Amy decided to stop by Lief's office to show him how it all looked.

Lief was in the lab when she arrived, mashing up fish samples. "Look who's here!" he said.

As soon as Amy saw him, she got that disappointed feeling again . . . like she was seeing a friend she no longer trusted. "We wanted to show you the issue," she said, handing it to him.

Across the banner Leah had drawn a special EARTH DAY logo. Underneath, the lead story headline read: "Toxic Levels of Mercury Discovered in Meramec River." Beside it was a photo of the sewage pipe they'd discovered.

Lief carefully read the mercury story and then flipped through the rest of the issue. "Nice, nice," he said, turning the pages. "Ah! You have a weather forecast?"

"My friend Grant put a weather station in our treehouse," said Amy. As it turned out, she hadn't had to say anything to Erin about her and Grant. It was obvious just by the way Grant was spending more time with them all, especially when Amy was around.

Now Amy watched as Lief read the movie review. Not a word. He closed the paper and looked up. "So. I think it's a fine job. How about you?"

"We think it's fine, too." Amy swallowed. "There's one thing that's really bothering me."

"What's that?"

"Well . . . if we were grown-ups and we were from a real newspaper, would you still have tried to fool us with the figures?"

Lief looked down at the lab counter. "I plan to give the *Post-Dispatch* the same information I gave you. And yes, I would have tried the same thing had you been adults." He paused. "This whole matter is bugging you, isn't it?"

"Sort of," said Amy. "Do you really think changing the figures is going to make that big a difference?"

He smiled. "I wouldn't have done it otherwise. I'll probably end up losing my job when they find out."

"Then why are you doing it?"

"Amy, this isn't about you and me or me and any other reporter, grown-up or otherwise. This is just my way of trying to help the river."

"But it's still lying," said Amy stubbornly.

"For a good cause," said Lief.

"I wish you could have thought of another way, then," said Amy.

Lief stopped for a moment. "Would you have been more comfortable printing the figures the other way?"

"Yes," said Amy. "But I'm not going to."

Now it was Lief's turn to look surprised.

"We're doing it your way, because of the river."

Lief put out his hand. "Thank you. Can we still be friends? Even though you don't like my tactics?"

"Okay," she said. She shook his hand. "I'm glad I talked to you."

"Me, too," said Lief.

Amy knew this issue was going to get a lot of attention when it came out, but she wasn't expecting the explosion of publicity when it actually happened. Naturally, everyone was shocked to read about the mercury contamination, and the phone started ringing almost as soon as all the papers were delivered.

One of the first calls was from Vicky at the *Post-Dispatch*. "You've done it again!" she said. "I brought a copy of the paper into work and everyone is talking about your lead story." Then she added, "It looks as if Lief's plan is working."

"I know," said Amy.

Vicky went on. "By the way, when Lief called here yesterday, he gave us the same contamination figures he gave you. Then when the reporter assigned to the story called Lectro, the plant said the contamination was exaggerated, which of course no one believed. The local Environmental Action Group was outraged. They plan to picket next week."

Amy half-smiled. "What about the rest of the issue?"

"I thought it looked good. Why?"

"Did the movie review bother you?"

Vicky laughed. "Not really. It wasn't your usual movie fare, but that's okay."

Amy hesitated. "Vicky? Do you think anything bad is going to happen to Lief for lying?"

"I don't know. If they figure out he did it deliberately he might lose his job. I guess that's a risk he decided to take, though, wasn't it?"

"Yeah," said Amy. "It was."

Later that afternoon Amy was in the treehouse straightening out her papers when Grant showed up to check on his weather instruments. "Hi," she said, quickly patting down her cheeks. "Thanks for helping with the papers this morning."

Grant had on a new ZZ ROCK T-shirt that made him seem like a roadie instead of a mad inventor. Erin had once told Amy she thought his looks had been improving since Thanksgiving, and Amy decided she was right. "Whew," he said, wiping his forehead with a bandana. "I can't believe how much people are talking about the paper." The way he said it almost sounded like he considered himself part of things . . . well, maybe he *was* part of things lately. He squinted his eyes and looked out the window. "Uh-oh. More low-lying clouds." He ambled over to record them on his chart.

"What's that mean?" said Amy.

Grant checked his barometer. "Well, if the air pressure starts falling, which it is, and the wind comes from the east . . ." He craned his neck out the window. ". . . which it is, then supposedly rain is on the way."

Amy shook her head. "Which wipes out all the Earth Day celebrations tomorrow."

Grant scribbled some notes on his weather chart. "Maybe not. I don't think the rain will show up until late evening." Then without looking up from the chart he added, "I'm going to a free concert in Emerson Park tomorrow. Want to come? Assuming it's not raining, naturally."

Her stomach went ker-thump. She was sure her cheeks looked like polished apples. "I'll have to ask my parents." Then she added, "But they'll probably say yes since it has to do with Earth Day."

Grant looked at her. "It's good to get your mind off the paper once in a while."

Amy smiled. "You know something, Grant? I think you're right."